This Book Belongs to:

The Borgese Family, with ♡

From:

Mrs. Baruffi

Date:

5/6/17

Clarence

The Story of a Boy
With Big Ears and a
Big Italian Family

Written by Stephanie Baruffi

Illustrated by Michela Cardelli

Foundations, LLC.
Brandon, MS 39047
www.FoundationsBooks.net

Clarence
Written by Stephanie Baruffi

Illustrated by Michela Cardelli

ISBN: **978-1544671680**
Cover by Michela Cardelli Copyright © 2017

Edited and Formatted by Laura Ranger

Copyright 2017© Stephanie Baruffi

Published in the United States of America
Worldwide Electronic & Digital Rights
Worldwide English Language Print Rights

Dedication

To the four loves of my life: Art, Jack, Luke, and Matthew #HomeTeam

To my BIG Italian family for making life so much fun!

To: Pop Pop, "Love, Susie"

Clarence stepped off the bus and heard someone yell from behind, "Bye, bye, big ears!"

He frowned and began to walk home.

Clarence was tired of all the kids at school making fun of his ears. Each day, they would take turns making jokes about him and calling him names.

Clarence felt discouraged, until he opened the front door. Instantly, a smile spread across his face, as he smelled "Nonna the Great's" meatballs. Clarence's family called his *Nonna* that because she was always in her garden, picking big tomatoes to make homemade gravy. She called herself "The Greatest of All Time," so the name stuck with her.

Clarence put down his book bag to follow the smell of meatballs, when Stella, the family dog, greeted him at the door. She licked him with her enormous tongue and slobbery mouth. "Ah, gross!" said Clarence. Although she was a bit much, Stella always had a way of making Clarence feel loved.

"Hi, *Nonna*!"

"Oh, *piccolino*, how was your day?"

"Eh, it was okay."

"Just *cosi-cosi*? *Perche*?"

"It's some kids at school. They are still making fun of me because of my big ears. They won't even let me sit with them on the bus."

Clarence washed his hands, as his mom came over to him and kissed him on his forehead. "How was your day, sunny?" She always called him that and Clarence liked it.

Daria, Clarence's sassy little sister walked in. "Oh, hi, sunny," she said in a smart tone.

"I heard that." Clarence replied.

"Of course you did. Your ears are enormous!" Daria laughed.

Joey, Clarence's tall, dark and handsome older brother strutted in. He smiled at Clarence and said, "We couldn't all get the good looks, kid. God must have given them all to me, so there was none left for you."

"Now, now kids. Don't talk to Clarence like that. Family **always** comes first. Never forget that," ma said.

Just as Daria rolled her eyes at ma's comment, Clarence heard the doorbell ring. It was his *Zio* and *Zia's* family. There were ten of them and they were loud! They came over almost every night for dinner and dessert. *Zia* Gina always made the zuccarinis and pizzelles for dessert. They both were Clarence's favorites!

Clarence's family gathered around the dinner table. At the head of the table sat Clarence's father, who had just finished a long day's work at the family business. After he prayed with the family, they dug into a delicious Italian meal that included chicken cutlets, homemade meatballs, and pasta fagioli. Each night during dinner, the family hollered back and forth across the table. Everyone talked in multiple conversations. Clarence watched and wondered why. He was a shy boy and didn't seem to understand why everyone shouted, especially all at once. As Clarence looked around the table, he noticed each member of his family had black hair, brown eyes and dark skin. He also realized all their ears were of normal size, and each of them seemed to look much like the other. But Clarence was the exception. He thought maybe the kids at school were right about him. This made him lose his appetite, so he asked to be excused. Nonna the Great followed Clarence into his bedroom.

Nonna said, "Sit down Clarence and let me tell you a story...

"Your *Nonno* had large ears, just like you. He had the most gorgeous blue eyes and golden blonde hair. That's why your momma named you after him. He too looked very different from the rest of his family. *Nonno* was a hardworking man who believed that no matter what, you should always believe in yourself. He would want you to believe that too. *Nonno* worked hard and started our family business. He was confident and didn't mind that he looked different from his family. He was proud to be Italian and proud of the way God made him."

Nonna the Great paused and said, "Wait here, I have something for you." Clarence waited as she retrieved something from her closet.

"Clarence, inside this box is something your grandfather carried with him when he traveled to America." The box was little, and inside was a delicate silver bell. *Nonna* said, "This tiny bell and the clothes on his back, were the only things *Nonno* had with him when he arrived at Ellis Island in 1912. When he was a small boy, his papa gave it to him to play with. It was then that *Nonno* saw his reflection in the bell, and realized he looked different from his family too.

"As *Nonno* grew into a young man, he kept that bell with him. He grew to love the reflection he saw in it each time he held it in his hands."

Clarence picked up the frail bell and thought about how the smell reminded him of an old library book. It made Clarence feel a connection to *Nonno* and that made him happy, especially because he never had a chance to meet his *Nonno*, who died before he was born. Clarence's blue eyes filled with tears.

Nonna held his chin and said, "I want you to have this in case you ever need to remind yourself that you are beautifully and wonderfully made. Be strong and confident in yourself."

Clarence hugged *Nonna* and wiped his eyes.

The next day, Clarence packed his book bag for school and put the silver bell inside. He thought maybe somehow, some way the bell would give him confidence.

Clarence climbed on the big yellow bus and sat in the first seat. Before long, a group of kids sitting in the back slowly crept up the aisle and sat behind him. A kid named Vinny yelled, "Hey big ears, wanna *hear* a joke?"

Giovanna laughed. "Good one Vinny, but you don't have to talk so loudly. With those ears, he could hear you a mile away!"

Clarence reached into his book bag and held his silver bell. He heard his *Nonna's* voice say, "Remember, you are beautifully and wonderfully made. Be confident in who you are." Clarence ignored the kids who were laughing at him and, before he knew it, they arrived at school. Clarence ran off the bus clutching his book bag and the bell that was tucked inside.

Clarence sat alone at school. He was used to it. He watched the other children laugh at each other's jokes and found himself wishing he could be a part of it. He reached inside his book bag to grab the bell. He tucked it into his pocket, as his teacher, Mrs. Matthews called the class to meet on the carpet.

Giovanna and Vinny pushed past Clarence to sit down. Giovanna whispered, "We don't want you in our group, so don't even bother to try and sit with us."

Vinny nodded. "Yeah, big ears. Sit by yourself."

Clarence didn't understand how people could be so mean.

He reached into his pocket, quietly slid the bell out and gazed at it. He saw his reflection, just like *Nonno* had done when he was a boy. Somehow, some way, Clarence saw himself differently. He leaned in a little closer and looked deeply into the glossy bell. His ears didn't seem that big at all. He thought about what Nonna the Great said and it started to make sense. He suddenly felt confident and brave and he knew what he had to do next.

Mrs. Matthews checked her wristwatch. "Okay students, it's time for recess."

The students headed outside to the large wooden playground. As usual, Clarence walked around the playground alone. That is, until Giovanna and Vinny pushed him from behind. Clarence turned to face them. Vinny grabbed Clarence by the shoulders and pushed him again. This time, Clarence flew backward and hit his back against a wooden pole near the slide. Clarence began to get angry, but then he took a deep breath. He realized this was his chance. He was finally able to say what he wanted to for so long.

Clarence looked Giovanna in the eyes and said, "Did you know you have like, 100 orange freckles on your face, but I have never said anything about those? And Vinny, your bifocals make your eyes look like tiny marbles, but that doesn't matter to me. I never pointed that out to you because it doesn't matter. You hurt my feelings every day and I am tired of it!"

Giovanna huffed, as Vinny's eyes started to fill with tears. He stepped away from Clarence slowly, then turned and ran. From a distance, Clarence could hear Vinny crying to Mrs. Matthews about what had happened. Before he knew it, Clarence saw Mrs. Matthews approaching him with Vinny close behind. She stopped in front of Clarence and Giovanna. "You three will be spending lunchtime with me."

Giovanna turned and stuck her tongue out at Clarence.

The students retrieved their lunches from the cafeteria, then Mrs. Matthews took Clarence, Vinny and Giovanna back outside, to sit on a bench in the school's courtyard. Mrs. Matthews turned to the children and said, "I have noticed you are struggling to take care of each other and respect each other's feelings. Let's talk about how we can be kind to one another and make smart choices."

All three students sat quietly for several minutes. Clarence thought about how his mom said family always comes first. He also thought about Mrs. Matthews always telling them they were part of a school family. Clarence said, "Mrs. Matthews, being part of a family means being kind, respecting each other and loving one another."

Vinny realized what Clarence said was true. Vinny looked at Clarence and said, "I'm sorry for the way I have been treating you."

Mrs. Matthews smiled, "Giovanna, would you like to say something?"

Giovanna quickly replied, "Nope."

Mrs. Matthews praised the boys for thinking about their words, and asked them to come up with something they could do together. Mrs. Matthews let the boys go play and made Giovanna sit and talk more about her attitude.

Clarence arrived home from school. He couldn't wait to tell *Nonna* what had happened. As usual, she was cooking in the kitchen. Clarence ran in yelling, "*Nonna*, guess what happened?" Before she could respond, Clarence began, "Today I used my bell to help me feel brave and stand up for myself! Mrs. Matthews talked to Vinny, Giovanna and I about speaking kindly to each other. Then Vinny asked me to sit with him on the bus tomorrow morning."

"Oh, *piccolino*, I am so proud of you. I knew somehow, some way you would realize you are brave. You are a special part of our family and your *Nonno* would be so proud!"

Clarence blushed. "Thanks, *Nonna*. Now if you don't mind, I would love some meatballs. I missed out on them last night."

"*Andiamo!*" *Nonna* replied as she set a plate out for Clarence.

Before he even brought a meatball to his mouth, his big, loud family filled the table, once again. This time as Clarence looked around the table, he didn't feel so different. He knew in his heart that, although he may have different colored eyes and bigger ears, he was part of something wonderful; his family. From that day on, Clarence understood he was beautifully and wonderfully made, just like his *Nonna* said.

And like almost every night before then, his family shared stories, passed food and enjoyed each other's company, like big Italian families do. And this time, Clarence even joined in!

Guide for Italian meanings

ITALIAN WORDS FROM THE STORY:

1. **PICCOLINO** - MEANS "LITTLE ONE"
2. **PIZZELLES** - TRADITIONAL ITALIAN WAFFLE COOKIES MADE FROM FLOUR, EGGS, SUGAR, BUTTER AND VEGETABLE OIL.

3. **ZUCCARINIS** - ANISE FLAVORED ITALIAN KNOTTED SUGAR COOKIE TOPPED WITH ICING
4. **COSI-COSI** - TERMS USED TO DESCRIBE A FEELING "SO-SO"
5. **PERCHE'** A WORD IN ITALIAN THAT MEANS, "WHY?"

6. **NONNA** - ITALIAN WORD THAT MEANS GRANDMOTHER
7. **NONNO** - ITALIAN WORD THAT MEANS GRANDFATHER
8. **ELLIS ISLAND** - LOCATED IN THE UPPER NEW YORK BAY IT WAS THE GATEWAY FOR OVER 12 MILLION IMMIGRENTS TO THE UNITED STATES AS THE NATION'S BUSIEST IMMIGRANT INSPECTION STATION FROM 1892 UNTIL 1954
9. **ZIO** ITALIAN WORD THAT MEANS UNCLE

10. **ZIA** - ITALIAN WORD THAT MEANS AUNT
11. **ANDIAMO!** ITALIAN WORD THAT MEANS "LET'S GO"

About the Author

I'm from New Jersey where I live with my husband, Art and three sons. In 2003, I began to pursue my education degree. I graduated from The Richard Stockton College with a bachelor's degree. Art and I married in 2005 and between 2007 and 2010, I gave birth to our three sons. With that, came so much joy and responsibility, we decided I'd resign and stay home with them. It was in those years, God revealed a desire to write children's books. Even though this dream was increasing each day, I put it on hold because being a Mommy to "3 under 3" was exhausting!

When the boys were a little older, I began to teach night classes at Cumberland County College. During this time, I decided to pursue my Master's Degree in Reading. In 2014, I earned that degree from Rowan University, along with my Reading Specialist Certification, graduating Summa Cum Laude.

Currently, I am an Early Literacy Specialist at Children's Literacy Initiative in Pennsylvania. For more than four years I have eagerly awaited the birth of Clarence! It was a true labor of love and I hope you enjoy sharing it with your family and friends!

Acknowledgements

I would like to thank Michela Cardelli for beautifully illustrating the characters in the story. You brought to life characters that mean so much to me, and for your tireless dedication I say, "Grazie."

I would also like to thank Laura and Toni at Foundations, LLC for your direction and putting the finishing touches on this project.

I would like to thank my family for instilling in me values that matter most: loyalty, love and laughter. Because of you all (and there are so many), I am the luckiest girl in the world!

Most of all—thank you PopPop. Your presence in my life can never be replaced, duplicated or forgotten. For the rest of my days, I will hold you deep inside my heart.

Principal Kidd: School Rules!
By Connie Colón

What happens when an 11-year-old, with a chicken for a sidekick, becomes the principal of an elementary school?

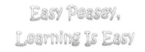

Easy Peasey, Learning is Easy
By Alissa B. Gregory

Fun, colorful book to help children learn, their alphabet, colors, numbers and shapes.

School's Not So Bad
By Alissa B. Gregory

Go along with Mary Ellen on her first day of school, to discover school's not so bad.